Nightmare Hill

by Michèle Dufresne

Pioneer Valley Educational Press, Inc.

On Monday, Amanda said,
"Let's go sledding
on Nightmare Hill."

"No," said Sam.
"Let's play on the tire swing."

On Tuesday, Amanda said,
"Let's go sledding
on Nightmare Hill.
It will be fun!"

"No," said Sam.
"Let's make a snowman."

On Wednesday, Amanda said,
"Let's go sledding
on Nightmare Hill.
It will be fun.
We can go fast!"

"No," said Sam.
"Let's play on the slide."

On Thursday, Amanda said,
"Let's go sledding
on Nightmare Hill.
It will be fun.
We can go fast
down the hill!"

"No," said Sam.
"Let's make snow angels
in the snow."

On Friday, Amanda said,
"Let's go sledding
on Nightmare Hill.
Come on, please!"

"OK," said Sam.
"We will go sledding
on Nightmare Hill."

"This is fun!" shouted Amanda.

"Aaaah!" said Sam.
"Aaaah!"